Discover the **DARK ENCHANTMENT** series

Other titles in the **DARK ENCHANTMENT** series

The Lost Brides

THERESA RADCLIFFE

PUFFIN BOOKS

PUFFIN BOOKS

Published by the Penguin Group
Penguin Books Ltd, 27 Wrights Lane, London w8 5TZ, England
Penguin Books USA Inc., 375 Hudson Street, New York, New York 10014, USA
Penguin Books Australia Ltd, Ringwood, Victoria, Australia
Penguin Books Canada Ltd, 10 Alcorn Avenue, Toronto, Ontario, Canada M4V 3B2
Penguin Books (NZ) Ltd, 182–190 Wairau Road, Auckland 10, New Zealand

Penguin Books Ltd, Registered Offices: Harmondsworth, Middlesex, England

First published 1996
1 3 5 7 9 10 8 6 4 2

The author wishes to acknowledge 'The Ruins of the Abbey of Fitz-
Martin' and 'The Bleeding Nun of St Catherine's' (from *Romances and
Gothic Tales*, 1801) republished in *The Oxford Book of Gothic Tales*,
Chris Baldick, 1993.

The moral right of the author has been asserted

Typeset by Datix International Ltd, Bungay, Suffolk
Printed in England by Clays Ltd, St Ives plc
Set in 12/14 pt Monophoto Sabon

CHAPTER I

CATHERINE STARED OUT of the carriage window. The rolling wooded hillsides had given way to bleak moorland. Birds flew up from the coarse grass as the carriage lurched its way along the rutted highways. At first the rough jolting of the carriage had made her sick. Now, after three days, she'd grown used to the swaying motion, but she still found it hard to sleep.

It had grown colder and colder the further north they'd travelled. Catherine pulled the fur wraps tightly round herself, nestling closer to Blanche. They had eaten well at the last inn and her old nurse was sleeping comfortably.

The rocking of the carriage was almost a comfort to her now, as though she was a child in a cradle. But the thought brought her mother's face back to her, and she felt tears sting her eyes. Everything she had known and loved was gone, and so quickly. Of her past life, only Blanche was left. Her future lay in the hands of this huge man, this stranger who sat opposite them.

He, too, was sleeping. She watched his stomach rise and fall. The air whistled out of his mouth in little gasps and snorts. His breath was sweet and sickly from the cloves he chewed to ease his aching teeth. Catherine found herself turning her face from him each time he bent forward to speak or whisper in her ear.

The man was Catherine's uncle, Sir Robert Helmsby, her mother's elder brother. Her mother had married a young lawyer with no connections or fortune and she'd been cut off by her family. Catherine had only met her uncle once before, three days after her mother's death. The plague had swept through their part of London, taking Catherine's mother and father within two days of each other. Catherine's dying mother had written to her brother, begging him to take in her orphaned child.

Sir Robert Helmsby, having seen the beautiful, dark-haired girl, knew at once that here was something which could be put to his advantage. Having no children of his own, this girl might be his one way out of his present difficulties, the lever he had been looking for to find favour with the new King.

The timing was perfect. Robert Helmsby was tired of life in London. He was denied access to the Court; his main estates had been confiscated. He would move north, take up the small, forgotten inheritance that had been his family's for generations. There he would find a suitable match for the girl among the King's supporters.

So it was that only weeks after her parents' death, Catherine found herself travelling towards some unknown place, with a man who was a stranger to her and only her old nurse for a companion.

Although partly repelled by him, Catherine couldn't help being grateful to her uncle for the kindness and attention he seemed to show her. By the time the long and difficult journey was nearly over, Catherine had begun to warm to him and feel fortunate that she had not been left completely alone in the world.

As the pace of the carriage began to change, Catherine leant again towards the window. The horses seemed to be labouring, pulling slower as the highway climbed upwards. The wind had risen and dark clouds were gathering over the moor, hanging like a black-purple blanket above them. Rain fell, huge drops lashing the road, turning the dust to rivers of mud in moments. The tired horses began to slip in the ruts, losing their footing.

Suddenly the carriage stopped and Joseph appeared at the window. Joseph had worked for Sir Robert for many years and, apart from the coachman, was the only servant Sir Robert had brought. The noise of the growing storm was deafening. Joseph had to shout above the wind.

'We'll get no further in this. We'll not cross these moors safely tonight. The night's closing in fast. There's a light up ahead, we'd better stop there.'

The carriage pulled away again and Catherine stared out into the rain and the growing gloom – the bleak building ahead didn't look very promising.

As they drew up, two huge mastiffs ran towards them, barking at the carriage wheels. Joseph jumped down, whipping the snarling beasts away. A rough-looking man hurriedly appeared with a lantern.

They entered a low, dismal room with smoke-blackened walls. The only light came from a small fire glimmering in the hearth which the torrents of rain down the chimney threatened to put out. The landlord ran round like a madman, bellowing to a bewildered girl to bring in more logs and lights. Catherine stood shivering by the fire.

At last, a table and benches were cleared in front of the fire and they sat down. Sir Robert ordered a round of ale for the two dislodged locals, whose sullen glares were soon replaced by friendly nods. As the fire took hold and the lights lit, the whole room took on a more cheerful appearance.

Bread and hard cheese were brought them and a plate of meat. Catherine ate little but Blanche and Sir Robert dined well. When Sir Robert had finished eating and drinking he felt ready to talk, and called the landlord. 'My coachman will need directions for tomorrow. We don't know this part of the country well.'

'Where are you heading, Sir?'

'Helmsby.'

'Helmsby?' The man looked puzzled. 'The Helmsby beyond Norton?'

Sir Robert nodded.

'There's nothing there now but the village.'

'We are going to Helmsby Abbey. You know it perhaps?'

The man looked astounded. 'The ruins?'

'The Abbey is my family seat. I intend to restore it to its former splendour.'

The flustered landlord turned to the locals. 'Can either of you direct this gentleman the best way to Helmsby Abbey? I don't know that way myself, not beyond Norton.'

Catherine had been listening intently to the conversation. 'What does he mean, Uncle, ruins? What are these ruins?'

'Indeed, my dear, I believe that the old Abbey is somewhat run down. I remember my father saying that it hadn't been lived in for a long time, since part of it was damaged by a fire.'

One of the men had crept closer to the party. 'Not lived in, Sir, not in my lifetime, nor my father's, nor my father's father's. Not by a human thing. No one ever goes near the old Abbey now. My wife's family is from that way. She has a sister still at Helmsby.'

'Perhaps you have heard of my steward then,

Norman Clare? His family has looked after the estate for some generations. Is he still living?'

'There is a Norman Clare, landlord of the White Hart, Helmsby. You'll be staying there I expect?'

'Indeed not, we shall take up residence at the Abbey immediately.' Seeing the sudden look of horror and disbelief on the man's face, Sir Robert wanted to be rid of him. He pressed a coin into his hand and asked him to find Joseph and the coachman in the stables and give them directions for the morning.

That night as Catherine lay on a rough mattress trying to sleep, the look on the man's face came back to her. She lay there listening to the wind, remembering what he had said, 'not lived in ... not by a human thing ...', wondering what he had meant, wondering what the next day would bring.

CHAPTER II

HALF A DAY'S journey should have taken them to the Abbey, which lay at the top of the steep wooded slopes above the village of Helmsby. The River Helm ran along the valley floor. It was a gentle, tinkling stream at the height of summer, but with the autumn rains or the melting snows it became a fast-flowing, raging torrent, sweeping over the treacherous rocks which lay on the river bed below the Abbey.

They made good time over the moors, despite the mud-soaked road. The day was clear and bright. Another month or two with the winter snows and even this highway across the moors would be impassable.

At Norton they turned off the main highway and began to make their way along rutted tracks more often used by farm carts and single horses than covered carriages. Their progress became very slow. As they began the perilous climb up the steep slopes towards the Abbey, it seemed that they would never arrive in daylight. Time and again Joseph and Martins the coachman had to jump down to put bracken under the wheels, which spun hopelessly in the soft

7

ground, or to hack away the undergrowth which had crept over the little-used track. The track zigzagged up the steep side of the wooded ravine and it seemed to the occupants of the carriage, as they peered anxiously out of the windows, that at any moment they would topple off the path and be dashed to the rocks below.

Catherine felt a growing excitement. The forest seemed huge, dark, forbidding. It seemed to be swallowing them up. Far above them, through the trees, she caught glimpses of white stone glinting in the evening sun. Higher and higher they climbed as the shadows lengthened. At last the ground levelled out and, as they entered a wide, treeless avenue, the full magnificence and splendour of the crumbling Abbey were revealed.

The ruins towered above them, gaping turrets and battlements, broken casements, great stone arches and columns rising up from the forest floor. Ivy and wild clematis covered the crumbling masonry, climbing and cascading over the outer walls. And higher than all rose a blackened tower, a dark, ominous presence keeping watch over the silent Abbey.

They climbed out of the carriage and stood staring upwards. Even Sir Robert seemed lost for words. Blanche crossed herself and stood open-mouthed, pointing at the terrible edifice before them. Catherine would remember the strange stillness of that moment. No sound came from the forest, no birds singing, no wind rustling the leaves. Only the laboured panting of the horses and the distant roar of the river far below. The evening sky had suddenly grown dark and heavy and there was not a breath in the air.

Then suddenly the cry, the screech of an owl, broke the silence. An owl leaving its nest in the ruined tower to go hunting, swooping down towards them, gliding silently on white wings, talons outstretched. And at that moment a jagged flash of lightning tore the sky, and thunder shook the tottering buildings. The owl flew over them, clipping Martins on the shoulder and the coachman fell to the ground in a gibbering heap. Huge drops of rain began to fall from the dark sky.

Catherine and Blanche ran for their cloaks, while Joseph tried to help the coachman to his feet. He turned to Sir Robert. 'We'd better make our way down to the village and find rooms there.'

Sir Robert shook his head. He would not be put off. 'Nonsense. In any case, we wouldn't make it to the village in daylight and a storm is breaking. We must quickly find our way into this place before night falls and seek what shelter we can, unless we are to stay in this carriage all night.' He pointed to the coachman, who was still on the ground, shivering, with his head in his hands. 'Whatever's the matter with the man?'

'Last night at the inn they filled his head with tales of apparitions and spectres and such things,' said Joseph.

'Leave him here with the horses.'

Taking Catherine's arm, Sir Robert said, 'Come, my dear, the rest of us will try to get in through this main gate ahead.'

The huge wooden gate creaked slowly open as Sir Robert and Joseph tried their full weight against it. It opened on to an inner courtyard. The forest had found its way even inside these walls. Brambles and ivy covered the ground, but some of the buildings around the courtyard looked in considerably better condition than the Abbey had first appeared. The tall, blackened tower was indeed in a terrible state of decay, as was the great vaulted nave of the church which was open to the sky. However, other buildings and covered galleries looked undamaged.

The rain was now falling very heavily and the terrific thunder threatened to bring down the crumbling tower upon them any moment. They hurried for the nearest doorway. To their surprise the door opened easily and they found themselves standing on the threshold of a great hall.

The walls and roof of the chamber were still intact and no vegetation had found its way inside. On the walls and floors were fine coverings and hangings, cobwebbed and tattered now but evidence of past splendour. A damp, dark smell filled the air and the walls and furnishings dripped with mould. But despite its dilapidated state it wasn't hard to imagine that this had once been a magnificent banqueting hall.

The huge fireplace on one wall was soon filled with logs Joseph had found. In no time at all a roaring fire of scented oak and elm was helping to dispel the dank, musty odour of the place. Blanche and Catherine dragged the couches around the fire, laying clean cloaks and furs over them. The door was fastened against the growing gloom and whatever else might lurk in the forest. The exhausted travellers prepared for their first night at Helmsby Abbey, and settled down to sleep.

Only Catherine lay awake for a time, staring at the flickering flames in the hearth and the shadows on the walls, listening as the wind grew and howled around the ruins, expecting at any moment to see some gruesome spectre rise up and walk the floors. But at last she, too, fell asleep.

That night the old Abbey kept its secrets to itself. Nothing stirred or moved. No beast or dreadful apparition disturbed the sleep or dreams of the tired travellers.

CHAPTER III

As soon as it was light, Joseph set off with one of the horses down to the village to find Norman Clare. He was to bring back food and provisions and tell the steward that the lord of the estate had returned and wanted to see him immediately. Sir Robert gave instructions that Norman Clare was to hire and bring with him all the servants and workmen he could find. They were to begin restoring the Abbey at once.

Joseph found the White Hart quite easily but had a harder job convincing Norman Clare and his wife of his mission. Norman Clare's wife looked as though she had seen a ghost. Only after a great deal of prodding and poking and cries of 'Heaven deliver us' did she accept that Joseph was indeed real and had actually spent a night at the Abbey. They took Joseph in by the fire and brought him food and drink while he explained his master's wishes.

Norman Clare, like his father before him, had dutifully collected all the rents and tithes owing to the lord of the manor. The accounts were in good order and the money stored up, and the steward had no qualms about meeting the new lord. His wife would prepare a basket of provisions immediately and Norman Clare said he would follow shortly, bringing with him all the help he could.

'You'll not catch me up there, not after dark at any rate,' muttered Clare's wife as she prepared the basket.

'Servants will have to be found in the village,' said Clare.

'Maybe,' replied his wife, 'for the daytime, but no one will stop there at night. Doesn't that poor nun roam the ruins each night and doesn't the wicked Count himself run from top to bottom with all the flames of Hell pursuing him? No one has slept in that place for more than a hundred years.'

'Be quiet,' said Norman Clare, pointing to Joseph, who was looking pale. 'This poor man's just spent a night there and he's survived, hasn't he?'

While Joseph returned to the Abbey, Norman Clare began to make preparations. Word spread quickly that the lord of the estates had returned and there was soon a large crowd at the White Hart. Having worked their land and cared for their sheep for so many years without interference, the people didn't welcome their lord's return.

A long and fearful mistrust existed between the villagers and the Abbey. There was something evil about the place. The Abbey and its masters meant misfortune and disaster, and the villagers would have preferred to have nothing to do with it. Norman Clare did his best to reassure them that they would probably all do very well out of their lord's return, for Sir Robert needed servants and workmen quickly and would pay good money. However, he himself was troubled and, just as his wife had predicted, although many villagers were prepared to work at the Abbey during the day, none were willing to spend a night there. They had lived for too long with the stories and legends. As children, their parents had taken them from their beds when the moon was full, pointing to the ghostly ruins to show them where they would be sent if they weren't good.

What dark truths lay behind the legends? What mysteries and hidden secrets had given rise to these fearful tales of ghosts which stalked the ruins? A few older men in the village perhaps knew more than they would tell, terrible stories of dark times and darker deeds handed down from father to son, each sworn to secrecy.

Joseph returned to the Abbey with fresh bread and milk to find the company in good spirits. They had woken to find a heavy dew and mist covering the forest, but this had soon lifted to make way for a warm autumn day. A bright sun shone through the shedding trees, a golden carpet was beginning to cover the ground and the wild clematis now shone like silver garlands over the crumbling walls. Catherine was excited and enchanted by the wild beauty of the place. The Abbey had altogether lost the dark sinister feel of the previous night.

To his great relief, Sir Robert had discovered a number of large rooms adjoining the main hall. Although in a dilapidated state, their main fabric was intact and they could in a short time be made quite comfortable and elegant again. As for the rest of the Abbey, it was certainly beyond repair. He had tried to explore down a narrow passage leading off the main church. A number of doors along this gallery might have led to suitable servants' rooms, but behind them he discovered only weak and dangerous recesses. These were the former cells of the monastery, with flooring so decayed that it had in some places fallen in. As for the great tower, it was indeed a hollow, blackened shell which would not be worth restoring

On finding Joseph returned with the provisions, they settled down to eat and wait for Norman Clare to arrive with help from the village. Joseph at once began to tell the stories he'd heard about the nun and the old Count, forgetting for a moment that the Count was in fact an ancestor of his present master. Sir Robert quickly laughed at his apologies.

'There's not an abbey or castle round here that doesn't have some ghost or evil ancestor.

As we've all survived one night, I'm sure we'll survive many others.' He turned to Catherine. 'What do you think, my dear?'

'Even if there are ghosts, I'm sure we'll come to no harm. I'd like to know more about the poor nun though, if there ever really was such a person.'

'I don't think you'll have to wait,' said Sir Robert, pointing to a crowd of men and women struggling warily up a steep slope at the side of the Abbey. 'I'm sure these villagers will be able to tell you a few stories.'

The villagers hung together anxiously, keeping their distance until Norman Clare arrived with a cart and blacksmith along the main track. Then they set to work.

Leaving her uncle and Blanche to oversee the proceedings, Catherine crept quietly away to explore the woods below. She wanted to regain the peace and tranquillity of the morning. She wanted to be as far away as possible from all the noise and disturbance.

CHAPTER IV

THE GROUND WAS wet and sodden after three days of heavy rain. The only path Catherine could find was a trail worn through the undergrowth where some animal had pushed its way through the tangled vegetation. She could hear rushing water far below, and she made her way towards the sound. She hurried down the slopes, half scrambling, half slipping, breathless and eager to reach the river below.

The nearer she drew to the water, the darker the wood became. Lichen and moss covered the fallen trees and fungi fed on the decaying stumps. A dark, damp smell rose up. She was close now, almost there. She could see the river, flowing fast and furious. There was a sudden sound, a plop, as a little creature dived into the water. Catherine crept to the edge of the bank. Strange ferns grew up from the cold, damp earth. She peered down into the water, trying to discover what had made the noise. But the ground began to move – it was not earth but a mossy log on which she'd trodden. She was falling – she clutched desperately at the bank but could not regain her footing. She was in the water now. She cried out. The river was sweeping her away . . .

Further down the bank, the steward's son, William Clare, had been cutting willow. Here a bend in the river formed a deep, dark, natural pool and trees grew round on all sides. The willow was needed to make sheep pens that winter, but it was a place where none would linger, only visited when the need arose. Will hurried in his work. Like everyone who'd grown up in the village, he knew the dark tales and rumours surrounding the old Abbey. This pool which lay below the Abbey was known to them all as Owen's Pool.

A hundred years ago a boy had died here. His body had been found caught up against the large, jagged rock which rose from the centre of the pool. He had been the youngest son of the blacksmith, and had fallen in love with a girl from a noble family. The girl had refused to give him up and had been sent to the Abbey to repent her ways. The girl was never heard of again, and a few months later, Owen's drowned body was found in the pool. It was supposed that he had thrown himself into the water in anguish for his lost love. His ghost was believed to wander the banks calling for her.

The pool became a fearful place. For several years after his death, a number of young girls from the village were found dead in the same pool. It was said that they had been lured there by Owen's sad cries. They were called the Brides of Owen and had haunted the place ever since, calling others to their death. Even now, no one ever came near the pool after dusk.

Will had just finished gathering up his bundle when he heard Catherine's cry. He stood still for a moment, thinking at first that he had imagined it. It was hard not to come to the pool without the old stories running through your head. The place was dark and sombre and terribly still. He had been startled often enough by the cries of water birds which occasionally broke the silence.

The cry came again. It was no bird, he knew that. Someone was crying out. Will stood rigid. It was a girl's cry, but no girl from the village ever came here. His heart was beating fast. He felt sweat gather on his forehead. Had the Brides of Owen come for him? Were they calling to him? What weed-covered spectre would stretch its arms towards him, dragging him down below the water with its deadly embrace? He wanted to run.

The torrent was sweeping Catherine towards the pool. She struggled to keep her head above the water, but her sodden cloak and gown were dragging her under. She tried to grasp the low branches which hung over the river, but the current swept her on.

And then Will saw her. He no longer hesitated – this was no phantom. He dived into the water, and managed to grab Catherine's cloak as she was carried towards the rock in the middle of the pool. As she clung to him he thought they would both be dragged under.

The river carried them out of the pool and downstream, but Catherine was strong. Together they fought the current and managed at last to reach the bank. Will took her hand to help her up. They were both shaking. They sat for a moment on the ground without speaking, trying to regain their strength.

'You're not a ghost, then,' said Will at last.

'I would have drowned,' said Catherine.

'Maybe, but you're a strong swimmer. It was only your cloak dragging you under.'

Will stared at her, still not quite believing what had happened. 'Where are you from, if you've not come to haunt me?'

Catherine laughed and pointed to the Abbey.

'You are a ghost, then,' said Will.

'I must get back,' said Catherine. 'They'll be worried.'

'You can't go there on your own.'

'Come with me, then, we can get dry there. It's nearer than the village and my uncle will want to thank you.'

Will had left home at dawn to see to the sheep and had not yet heard of Sir Robert Helmsby's arrival. As they climbed back up through the trees, Catherine told him of her uncle's plans. Like the other villagers, Will found it hard to believe that anyone was actually going to live in the old Abbey.

'We'd better go quickly,' said Will, 'to keep warm.'

Hand in hand they clambered back up the slopes, each helping the other, and laughing and shivering together as they stumbled through the tangled undergrowth.

CHAPTER V

CATHERINE AND WILL soon dried out in front of the fire in the old hall. Sir Robert made a great fuss of them both. He shook Will warmly by the hand, promising to do anything he could in the future for the boy, in return for saving his niece's life.

Norman Clare stood quietly by the fire, watching his son with Catherine and Sir Robert. A shadow seemed to cross his face and he frowned. 'Excuse me, Sir Robert, but there's work to be done.'

'Of course, of course,' blustered Sir Robert, 'but we're very grateful to you both. I dread to think what might have happened if your son hadn't been there.'

'The river below the Abbey is treacherous,' said Norman Clare. 'It's taken many lives. Miss Catherine had better not wander down that way alone again.'

'But it's so beautiful and quiet down there,' said Catherine. 'Perhaps Will could take me there, to show me where it's safe. Please, Uncle.'

Sir Robert turned again to Norman Clare. 'Well, if your boy's ever free and you can spare him, I'd be pleased for him to guide Miss Catherine. What do you say, Will?'

Will blushed and nodded.

'You must excuse us now,' said Norman Clare, 'but there's a lot to be done yet before nightfall.'

As they left, Catherine called after them, 'Come back tomorrow, Will, or the next day.' Then she turned to her uncle, suddenly flinging her arms around him. 'It's going to be all right here, I know it,' she cried, and ran out of the hall to find Blanche.

Blanche had been busy all morning cleaning out a small room with some of the village women. It was now nearly ready. The room had two small windows; one looked outwards to the forest and the other faced the inner courtyard and the dark tower beyond.

Catherine ran from one window to the other, her mind racing, unable to keep still for a moment. 'It's sad and strange here, Blanche, but I think I shall like it. There's so much to find out. Have you heard anything more about the nun? What did the villagers tell you? I want to know everything about the place.'

'Some things are better not known,' said Blanche, frowning. 'All this finding out and discovering – let the poor ghost alone.'

'So there really is a ghost? Do you believe it, Blanche?'

'Nobody knows for sure,' said Blanche. 'But even if there is, she won't do us any harm, I'm sure, poor creature.'

'Sister Anna?'

Blanche nodded. 'She was sent to the convent by her father because she refused to marry the Count and give up the boy she loved. Sent there until she should change her mind and do as her father wanted. But the poor child was never seen or heard of again.'

'The boy was called Owen. Will told me by the river. He drowned himself because he couldn't bear to live without her.'

'That's enough dead and dying for one day. These chests must be unpacked and Sir Robert will be calling us for supper.'

As evening approached the villagers all hurried away, despite Sir Robert's assurances that any who stayed would be paid well. However, a fine meal had been laid out in the hall and the fires lit. Sir Robert was in an excellent mood. The restoration looked likely to take less time than he'd first thought. Great improvements had been made after only one day's work. Things were turning out better than he'd dared hope.

When they had eaten, Blanche and Catherine left Sir Robert drinking in front of the fire and retired to their own room. After the wine and the day's work Blanche was ready to drop, but

Catherine was still eager to talk. She lay in bed, staring at the flickering candle.

'Why won't the villagers stay, Blanche? What are they frightened of? I don't think I shall be afraid if Sister Anna does come, but I wouldn't want to see the old Count, the one who died when lightning struck the tower, the one they tried to make poor Anna marry.'

'That was Count Drogo – it was he who had all the nuns turned out. I don't want him or anyone else disturbing my sleep, so not another word tonight. Blow out the candle.'

In a few minutes Blanche was snoring, and after a time Catherine fell asleep too. She hadn't been thinking about Count Drogo or Sister Anna or any ghosts at all, only about Will, wondering when she'd see him again and where he would take her.

Catherine woke suddenly. At least, she thought she was awake, but something seemed to be holding her back. It was as though she was in the water again, the dark pool. She seemed to be floating, drifting. She couldn't lift herself up. Everything she took hold of seemed to dissolve away. She was crying 'Help me, help me,' but the voice seemed far away, not her own. She was trying to keep her head above the water, to open her eyes, but her eyes wouldn't open.

At last she sat up. She stared around the room. She was certainly awake now, but she felt so cold and was shivering so much it was as though she really had been in the water again. She pulled the cover tightly around herself. Then she heard the voice again – it was still there. The voice wasn't inside her head at all, it was outside, a faint, distant crying, 'Help me, help me.'

Catherine ran to the window. The moon was shining down into the courtyard. Her eyes were drawn towards the tower, the dark ruin rising into the sky. It was from here that the cry was coming. For a second, she thought she saw something – a glimmer of white, a white shadow, a white figure disappearing into the blackness.

Catherine crept back to bed. She tried to sleep. Her heart was racing. What had she heard? What had she seen? Had she seen anything at all? She couldn't be sure. Was it Sister Anna calling to her? She was trembling now. She was frightened – not of ghosts or dreams, nothing as simple as that. It was something she couldn't grasp, just a feeling that chilled her. A feeling that something terrible had happened or was going to happen. As she lay there in the dark it was as though the walls themselves, the crumbling stones, were crying out to her, telling her what they had seen, warning what was to come.

That night, as the Abbey's first dark shadows crept into Catherine's mind, it was as though

all the light and promise of the day had disappeared. Only when the silver dawn flooded the
room did Catherine's muddled fears subside.

CHAPTER VI

THE NEXT MORNING, bright autumn sunshine bathed the old Abbey and quickly dispelled the troubled thoughts of the night. Only Catherine's bright feverish eyes betrayed her disturbed sleep. To Sir Robert, she looked more beautiful than ever. As he watched her run excitedly from room to room, he was certain that he had not made a mistake in coming to the place. The girl was captivating. As soon as the Abbey was fit to entertain in, he would have no trouble finding a suitable husband for her, whose connections would lead them back to civilization. The sooner the better, as far as he was concerned. After the previous night he wanted to get out of this godforsaken ruin as quickly as possible.

Sir Robert felt terrible. His head throbbed; he'd hardly slept at all. He too had woken up time and time again, gripped by some unspeakable fear which had left him shaking and trembling. Each time he had closed his eyes, his dreams had been the same. The face of the Count — presumably it was the old Count — staring down at him. The mad, bloodshot eyes, the screaming mouth, and all around the growing flames. A fire so real and terrible that it seemed to set his own bed alight. The covers felt like red-hot coals, smoke choked his nostrils, he could hardly breathe. When he woke his head was burning, sweat poured from his brow and screams still rang in his ears. In the morning he'd staggered exhausted from his bed.

Seeing his haggard, strained look, Blanche had asked if she should send for a doctor.

'Stop fussing,' growled Sir Robert. 'It's a touch of fever, that's all. If Norman Clare and the other men are here, send them to me. Let's get on with the work.'

As the day wore on, Sir Robert's temper improved. The weather was fine and Norman Clare organized the men efficiently. Large bonuses were promised if the work could be done before the snows came. Everyone who could be spared from the village came to help, including Will, who was set to work with the carpenter.

Catherine, too, was feeling better. The oppressive feelings of the night, the terrible sense of foreboding, had left her, but she felt strangely restless. She wandered for a time among the ruins. She was half repelled, half drawn to them. They fascinated her, she wanted to know more, yet at the same time she found herself wishing she was a hundred miles away. She wanted to be out in the open, away from the tower's dark shadow. She wished she was out in the forest with Will again.

Sir Robert had been alarmed to find Catherine wandering alone in the ruins. Fearing that the decaying masonry might fall on her, he told her to stay away. Explaining that she had little else to do, Catherine reminded her uncle of his promise and begged that Will should be released from his work to walk with her. Norman Clare was sent to find his son. He fetched him reluctantly and watched uneasily as Catherine and Will ran together towards the river path.

It was to be the first of many walks together. Catherine and Will slipped into an easy companionship. Will was happy to show her all the countryside he knew, Catherine was eager to explore and learn. They felt comfortable and happy together.

That first day, Will took Catherine upstream. For two or three miles they walked and clambered to where the river began as a tiny, fast-flowing trickle on the moors, far from Owen's Pool. They rested on open ground, high above the woods. A glimmer of white stone rising from the trees marked the distant Abbey. Will pointed. 'We don't seem to be able to get away from it, even here,' he said.

'It must have been beautiful once,' replied Catherine.

'Maybe, but it should have been left alone. No one's been near it for so long. They should have let it go back to the forest.'

'Perhaps it won't be so sad and gloomy when it's been restored.'

Will stared at the ground. 'I don't like thinking about you there. There's something strange about it, there always has been.'

Catherine looked at Will. She was quiet for a moment. She wanted to tell him what she had seen, what she had felt, but it was hard to put into words. 'I saw something last night, heard a voice – I'm not sure. This feeling came, it was something to do with her, with Sister Anna. I can't explain it, but something made me afraid. Not of her. It wasn't her trying to hurt me. It was more like a warning.'

Will found he was trembling. He clenched his fists tight. He didn't want to hear this. It worried him. His head had been filled with stories about the Abbey since he was small. Not even the most foolhardy boys in the village had dared to go near it. The place still made his spine tingle after dark. Although he hardly knew Catherine, he had felt close to her almost at once. He couldn't bear the thought of this or anything else happening to her at the Abbey. 'Be careful,' he whispered.

Catherine smiled. 'Don't look so serious, Will, you scare me. Perhaps I was only dreaming. It's just that in some strange way it seems as though she's connected to me. I don't think I shall be happy there until I find out what really happened to her. Doesn't anyone know?'

Will shook his head. 'She just disappeared. She may have still been with the nuns when they moved to another abbey near the coast. No one knows for sure. Her father tried to find her in the end. He wanted her to forgive him. But the nuns couldn't tell him where she was or what had happened to her.'

He stood up suddenly. He didn't want to think about Sister Anna any more. He didn't want to see Catherine serious and worried. He wanted to see her happy and laughing again. He hated the Abbey. 'Come on. We ought to go now, it's getting late. I'll race you back.'

They ran down the slopes, slipping and laughing as they fell. From time to time they stopped to gather mouthfuls of berries. The sun was setting by the time they reached the Abbey. Most of the villagers had left. Will's father was waiting for him. 'It's late,' he said gruffly to Will. He bowed stiffly to Catherine. 'Your uncle's waiting in the hall, Miss Catherine.'

CHAPTER VII

THOSE FIRST FEW weeks slipped by for Catherine like a dream. She bubbled over with excitement and happiness. The fine weather held. Only from time to time did thoughts of Sister Anna disturb her; for the most part her days and her dreams were only full of Will. The work on the Abbey progressed well and, whenever he could, Will slipped away to join Catherine. He showed her the Abbey's lands, long abandoned and wild now. 'These fields could be worked again one day,' he said, 'and the pastures. Hundreds of sheep once grazed here, not like our small flock on the moor.'

Catherine and Will spent many hours together. They explored the rest of the river, although they avoided Owen's Pool. They walked every inch of the moors and woods, gathering the wild plums and autumn fruits. Will taught Catherine everything he knew. He told her the names of the birds and small animals they saw busily collecting nuts and berries, preparing for the winter months ahead. They wandered a long way from the Abbey, for Catherine liked to sit watching and listening to the birds, the treecreeper and robin, the little wren and brightly coloured jay. During the day, the woods around the Abbey were silent, with no birdsong to be heard or scurrying animals to be seen. It seemed that only creatures of the night dared venture there.

Usually they kept clear of the village. The stares and glances of the villagers made them both feel uncomfortable. But once Will took Catherine to the old churchyard to show her where Owen, the blacksmith's son, was buried. The grave was set apart from the main burial ground, but there was a stone which bore his name.

Catherine stared sadly at the grave. 'He looks so alone here and he was so young when he died. They were together for such a short time, before she disappeared. He must have loved her very much.'

Will nodded. 'They say he tried to climb the Abbey walls once to find her.'

It had been colder that day and the sun was hidden behind the first mists. The rooks were circling high above them. Catherine shivered under the old yews, remembering Anna. She'd almost succeeded in pushing Sister Anna from her mind. Sometimes the voice came to her at night, but never so clearly as that first time. Sometimes she would wake for no reason, a rush of cold air slipping past her face, but in the morning she forgot again. The days had been so golden, so filled with excitement and with Will.

Will put his arm gently round her. 'It's getting cold and late, we'd better go.'

They walked back up to the Abbey without talking, hand in hand. Only when they reached the Abbey and saw Will's father approaching did they feel awkward and pull apart.

As the days grew shorter a change came. Will's father was unwilling to spare him and Catherine found herself more and more alone and strangely uneasy. The freedom and happiness she had known with Will seemed to be coming to an end. Thoughts of Sister Anna came often now; the long days and especially the nights filled her with dread. Sometimes she passed the time helping Blanche and the other women. There were still hangings and covers to be made, but she did not like to sit with them for long. At other times she had to undergo endless fittings, for her uncle had bought satins, linen and fine velvets, which were to be made into dresses and other garments for her. Catherine was not particularly interested in such finery and, although grateful to her uncle, begged him not to waste his money.

'But, my dear,' he explained, 'you're the lady of the manor now. Once the Abbey's apartments are finished we must take our place in society. There will be other knights and lords and ladies to entertain. You can't spend all your time roaming the woods and fields like a peasant. Be a good girl now and show me the green velvet.'

Catherine longed to walk with Will again, but she said no more. She didn't want to upset her uncle. She was beginning to discover how quickly and terribly his moods could change. Of them all, it was Sir Robert who seemed most affected by the Abbey. At times Catherine and the servants hardly knew him. In just those few weeks he had become like a madman: all smiles and sweetness one moment and then, at the slightest provocation, upturning tables and raining curses down on them.

Sir Robert's tortured nights had continued. The only comfort he could find was in wine and ale. He drank continuously – nothing else could block out the ghastly spectres that filled his dreams. At night they would hear him screaming through the Abbey as though pursued by demons. He slept with a sword by his side.

Catherine began to avoid her uncle whenever possible. She missed seeing Will terribly. She told herself it would be all right once the work was finished. She and Will would have time together again. It seemed that it was only his presence which kept her own nightmares at bay. Without him, the feeling had returned, the same intangible fear that something terrible was going to happen.

A hundred images seemed to fill her dreams. The fleeting figure of the nun calling again and again, 'Help me, help me,' the brides in the pool and she with them, their hideous green arms pulling her down. Sometimes she'd see Owen floating there, but as she gently turned the body she'd realize it was not Owen at all, but Will. Often she saw the dark tower and herself falling, falling into the blackness; only then it wasn't her, it was Sister Anna, white habit floating, screams echoing. What did it all mean? What was happening to her? Was she going mad too?

Catherine knew she had to find out more if she was to make sense of these fears, these feelings that haunted her. It was as though in some awful, unexplainable, inescapable way Sister Anna's fate was linked to her own, as though an invisible thread lay between them, drawing them closer and closer.

Catherine had seen Will only once since the day in the churchyard. She'd told him then that she was going to search the ruins. He'd listened to her white-faced, begging her to leave it, to put Sister Anna from her mind or at least to wait until he could help her.

'No, Will, I've got to do it. I can't wait any more. It's as though the place is closing in on me.'

He'd wanted to take hold of her then, to take her in his arms, to say something to comfort her, but Norman Clare had come at that moment and sent him back to work.

Catherine had tried several times to see Will again, to catch his eye as she walked past, but his head was always bowed to his work and she never found him alone. Only the thought of searching the ruins somehow kept her going. The idea obsessed her. If she found out the truth about Sister Anna, perhaps everything would be all right, perhaps the dreams and the fears would disappear.

Her uncle had forbidden her to wander in the most decayed and crumbling parts of the ruin, so Catherine knew she would have to wait for a time when he had left the Abbey. She couldn't risk being discovered; she must do nothing to cross him.

CHAPTER VIII

CATHERINE'S CHANCE CAME at last. The first frosts of autumn had arrived. The morning was cold and grey. The wild clematis on the outer wall glistened white and the twigs on the trees had turned to silver. It took a long time for the fire in the great hall to make any impression at all on the chill air. Catherine had risen shivering from her bed and had been surprised to find her uncle in unusually good spirits. The tired, haggard look which he wore each morning seemed to have left him. He was by the fire, pulling on his riding boots.

'I shall be gone all day, Catherine. One of our neighbours, Lord Osmund, has recently lost his wife and I must pay my respects to him.'

In fact, Sir Robert could hardly contain his excitement. The Osmund family was known to be favoured by the King. Lord Osmund spent part of each year at Court. Two previous wives had died childless. A beautiful, healthy young girl of good family, who could give him an heir, might be just what Lord Osmund was looking for. This was exactly the chance Sir Robert had been hoping for. That it should have come so soon was an extraordinary relief to him. The terrible nights in the Abbey were beyond belief. Normally a man of strong constitution, these fevers and nightmares which destroyed his sleep were more than he could bear. He just wanted to be rid of the place, get out of there at the first possible opportunity.

Joseph was waiting at the outer gate with the horses. Catherine watched Sir Robert ride off, relieved to see him go. Now at last she would be able to begin her search. Wrapping herself in her warmest cloak, Catherine slipped quietly into the inner courtyard. There was no one to disturb her – Blanche was still in her room. She walked slowly towards the tower. Its dark walls rose up above her. She wanted to turn back, to run, but she forced herself on. Wasn't it here that she'd seen the fleeting shadow, heard the cry? Surely this tower must hold the secret of Sister Anna's fate, and perhaps her own.

The tower was just as her uncle had described it: a decaying, blackened shell. The outer wooden door had gone. Catherine climbed some stone steps which led upwards inside the crumbling walls, but this stairway was soon blocked by fallen masonry and was completely impassable. She was forced to turn and follow the steps back down. She then discovered that, past the entrance, they led below the ground. The fire had not penetrated here. The walls, though dripping with mould and damp, were still intact and undamaged. The stone steps had been cut into the rock and were uneven and slippery.

Catherine clung to the wall, frightened that she would slip, wishing she had brought a light. She began to make her way slowly down towards the darkness. Five, six, seven steps she counted, and then seemed to find herself on a much wider step or landing. And suddenly her way was barred. In the dim light she could just make out a great iron grille. It had been set into the stairway, preventing any further access downwards. She took hold of the grille to move it, trying to lift it from its castings. She pulled hard but soon realized that it was far too heavy for her. To go further she would need help. She couldn't go on alone.

Catherine stood still for a moment, trying to catch her breath. There was a strange, unnatural silence about the place. She felt her heart beating. She listened, half expecting to hear the voice of Sister Anna calling to her. But there wasn't a sound. Not a breath of wind, not a leaf stirring, not a rustle – no movement of any living thing in that dark, underground place. It was the silence of death, the silence of a tomb. It was crushing her, overwhelming her, she couldn't breathe. She struggled to move. It was as though her feet were leaden, chained to the step. At last, she managed to turn. She saw a glimmer of daylight above her and ran up the steps towards it.

Catherine reached the courtyard. The clean, crisp air cut through her. She gasped, gulping it down into her lungs. She'd never felt so strange or so afraid before. It was as though the tower itself had been reaching out to swallow and smother her. As though it meant to keep her there for ever.

At last, she grew calmer, and began to breathe more quietly. She stared up at the cold, blue sky. She wasn't giving up. She'd have gone on then if the way hadn't been barred. She would come back to the tower and Will would come with her. Will would help her. But now there were other places to search, while she still had the chance.

A narrow passageway led off the main vaulted ruin of the church. Along this ruined gallery lay a number of crumbling recesses. Catherine would search here next. These were the lonely cells where the nuns had once lived and slept; perhaps she would find something here. At least these cells were not below the ground, they could not hold the same horror. The worst was surely over. She must hurry now before her uncle returned or Blanche came to find her.

She entered the main gallery through the ruined church. Although the passageway was dim, Catherine could make out the doors which led from it on either side. The wooden flooring of the cells was dangerously rotten in places and she had to tread with great care. The cells were almost bare – here and there she saw a single wooden cross hanging on a wall, a low bench. In each cell a single slit in the stone wall let in a trickle of light. Catherine searched each cell, her hands trembling with the cold, but she found nothing. Nothing at all which might enlighten her; nothing, that is, until she came to the last cell.

This cell was larger than the others. A small oak table stood in one corner. The cell was lighter, too, for there were two slits in the walls, one on the inner wall and the other on the outer forest wall. Outside the cold mist had lifted, and the autumn sun now streamed through this thin opening. As Catherine stared around the room, her eye was drawn again and again to the place where this ray of sunlight lingered on the far wall. She moved closer to inspect the stonework. One block of stone seemed to stand out further than the rest. As she moved her trembling hand slowly over it, the stone moved. It was loose. Gently, Catherine pulled it. It came away easily in her hand, revealing a small, dark recess inside the wall. A secret hiding place, perhaps? Her heart was beating fast now. Why was it there? What secrets did it hold?

The recess lay above Catherine's head, so she couldn't see directly into it. She stretched up and pushed her hand into the damp, dark hole. She strained, reaching further and further into it, pressing herself against the wall. On tiptoe now – nothing, just crumbling stone – and then her fingers touched something. Something smooth, damp and cold. Her fingers closed around it, and she drew back her hand. She held a piece of parchment, rolled and yellowing with age. It was very fragile but still intact. Catherine took it closer to the light; the writing on it was still clear and legible. Certain words stood out from all the others, '. . . Anna . . . Sister Anna'. She need search no further. Hiding it under her cloak, Catherine hurried away from the cell. She ran along the gallery and back to the hall, desperate now to reach there before Blanche stirred or her uncle returned.

Everything in the hall was bustle and noise. Blanche was in a great fuss because Catherine's green velvet dress hadn't been finished and Sir Robert had left instructions that it should be done that day. The dressmaker hadn't been able to find Catherine for a fitting.

Catherine quickly ran to her room and hid the parchment. She knew she would have no chance to read it until that night when Blanche was asleep. She returned to the hall in a daze. Nothing seemed real; she just wanted all of this, the whole day to be over so she could be alone.

Sir Robert came home in an excellent mood. Not only had Lord Osmund invited him to hunt the following day but he'd agreed to dine with them the following week. Sir Robert was anxious that Lord Osmund should see Catherine as soon as possible. Blanche protested that they were not ready yet for such entertaining, but Sir Robert would hear none of it. The hall was nearly finished and quite grand. If the kitchens weren't ready, the food could be prepared in the village and brought up. He would spare no expense. Swan, wild boar, partridges, sweetmeats and fine wine. Norman Clare was to organize it all. They might even hire musicians from the next village. Sir Robert talked and laughed and made plans until Catherine thought the evening would never end. She wasn't interested in any of it. Only one thing mattered to her now: Sister Anna and the letter she had found.

CHAPTER IX

NIGHT CAME AT last. Blanche and Sir Robert had eaten and drunk well and Blanche was now snoring comfortably in her bed. Carefully Catherine took out the parchment, unrolled it with trembling fingers and began to read by the light of the candle.

My hand is shaking although the night is warm. These things are almost too terrible to write, but write I must. Though sworn to secrecy, all of us, yet I cannot leave this thing untold. Should the Lady Abbess or Father Abbot find this – my confession – then I too will be condemned. Yet before God the truth must be told. This thing cannot be His will, that the young and innocent should so suffer for so unwilling a crime. To break our holy vows is indeed most terrible, but should the crime be met with such punishment as this? I pray to God to guide me.

Catherine was breathing very fast now. She felt cold sweat gather on her forehead, and forced herself to read on.

We took our sweet Sister Anna, half dragged, half carried her towards the tower under the stern command of the Lady Abbess. We had no choice, we dared not disobey, though her piteous cries rang in our ears. She begged forgiveness but the Abbess would not relent. Somehow we reached the tower. The great grille was lifted and we carried her to a dismal cell within. I tremble to recall that place, that place of final punishment. A coffin, black-draped and hideous, stood there, its cavernous mouth open to receive her. We had carried her not to confinement but to death. As we laid her on the cold floor she clung to us, pleading, eyes staring wildly round the cell, the horror slowly dawning. I begged the Mother Abbess to spare her, but she bade me be silent. She flung the girl from us and, fastening the door herself, drove us away.

We fled now back up the stone steps. The iron grille was lowered, for no one should pass that way again. No help or succour could we bring our sister. From that day hence we were forbidden even to speak her name, so terrible a disgrace was she said to have brought on the Abbey.

I do not know how we sisters carried on our duties and our prayers in the days that followed, all the while screams and cries echoing from that dreadful tower. Three days, four days, we begged the Abbess to relent and free her, but she would not. And then at last only silence; no cry, no sound came from that place and we knew that God had finally delivered her from torment. Poor Sister Anna was dead and, with her, her unborn child. Only I had known her secret. She had trusted and confided in me. Should I have stopped her taking her vows? Could I have saved her? How often I have asked myself that.

With shaking hands, Catherine read on. That night she learnt the full story of Anna's short life and death.

Anna had been banished to the Abbey by her cruel father until she should come to her senses and agree to marry Count Drogo. But it was a marriage that Anna could never undertake, for, unknown to her father, she was already married. She had been married in secret to Owen, the blacksmith's son, whom she had long loved. Anna had thought that in time her father would relent and let her leave the Abbey and be with the man she had chosen. But this was not to be. Count Drogo, on whose land the Abbey stood, was furious at Anna's refusal. He determined that if he could not have her then no one else would, nor was he prepared to wait. He instructed her father and the Lady Abbess that Anna must either take her holy vows or leave the Abbey and marry him at once.

Poor Anna could never marry Drogo. To tell the truth would have brought Count Drogo's wrath on Owen too. She had no choice but to take the holy vows. But she could not give up her lover, her husband of such a short time. She could not bear to be apart from him. At night she would slip away to meet him. No one inside the Abbey knew her secret but Count Drogo had many spies. One of them must have seen the two together, for somehow Count Drogo learnt the truth. Now was his chance, not only to punish the girl who had rejected him but to bring down the Abbess and the whole convent, which for many years he had been trying to destroy.

Count Drogo told the Abbess he had proof that the Abbey was not worthy, that one of the nun's had broken her holy vows, and said he would see that the order was disbanded. The proud Abbess haughtily dismissed his claims and demanded to see his evidence. But that night she found the evidence for herself. Sister Anna had fainted at the altar when the news of the Count's accusations had been given. She had been carried to her cell. As the Mother Abbess loosened Anna's clothing, she saw the proof of which Count Drogo had spoken: Sister Anna was going to have a child.

Poor Anna tried to tell the Abbess of her secret marriage. She begged for understanding and forgiveness but the cruel Abbess was set on one course alone – to save the convent. She would destroy this evidence, remove all shame from the Abbey. Sister Anna must disappear without trace.

Catherine looked up. The candle was spluttering gently now as though it would go out. She sat very still. She knew now what had happened to Anna, to Owen's lost bride. The truth was so awful, so simple, so obvious that it cut through her. Anna had loved Owen. Anna had refused to marry Count Drogo and because of this she had died a terrible death.

Catherine stared at the floor. She was shaking terribly. The nun's story had been so real, so vivid it was as though she had been there a hundred years before, had witnessed those events herself. She had found out the truth, but it made her feel no better. On the contrary, it was as though the nightmare was just beginning. She kept thinking about Will and then about Owen, poor Owen searching for his dead bride. Will ... Owen ... Owen ... Will ... the words seemed to be going round and round in her head.

She could see Will now, his smiling face. She wanted to be with him again, to be running and laughing and happy with him. These days without him had been unbearable. She didn't know what he felt about her, but she knew, she knew now that she loved him. And suddenly she knew too what she'd been so frightened of, the horror she had sensed. She understood the terrible feeling that had oppressed her since that night when she'd first heard the voice. Her own or Sister Anna's? It didn't matter now. They were the same. The fleeting figure by the tower? It was herself. What had happened here so long ago was going to happen all over again. The ruins, the crumbling stones, the long-dead spirits had screamed at her, warning her.

Catherine's head was spinning with the horror, the knowledge, the awful certainty . . . she was going to die like Sister Anna. Then, as she slipped finally into sleep there came a tiny glimmer of hope. She seemed to see two hands floating before her, two hands clasped in prayer, white as ivory, young and smooth like her own, and she felt their cold, gentle touch on her forehead.

CHAPTER X

THE NEXT MORNING Sir Robert left early for his day's hunting with Lord Osmund. Catherine slipped out. She was desperate to see Will now, she had to tell him what she had found. The workmen were already busy, carrying and cutting stone to repair the main outer wall. Will was among them. The men stopped, lifting their caps as she passed, which made Catherine feel uncomfortable. She smiled and nodded as graciously as she could. She didn't want to embarrass Will by going straight up to him in front of them. Then she caught sight of Norman Clare unloading some provisions from a waggon and ran to him.

'Please, I need to speak to Will. Let him stop work for a moment.'

Norman Clare looked at her, noticing how pale she seemed. He frowned. No good could come of any friendship between her and his son. The sooner Sir Robert got her married off the better. At the same time, he couldn't help feeling a little sorry for the girl, she was a good-natured child. Alone all day in those ruins it was no wonder she looked so pale, and it was hardly her fault she'd been born into such a family. Something was obviously worrying her. Against his better judgement he nodded and went to fetch Will.

'Miss Catherine wants to see you. Just a short time, now. I'd rather you were working, there's a lot to finish here, but I don't want her complaining to her uncle that we haven't been obliging.'

'She wouldn't do that, she's not like that.'

'Well, whatever she is, she's not for you. So just a short time now, and don't go far.'

Norman Clare watched them go. They walked side by side, slowly, as though deep in conversation. He sighed. He hoped Will wasn't already seriously interested in her. He would be glad when the work up here was finished. Once the snows came there would be little chance of much coming and going between the Abbey and the village. The girl would have to leave Will alone then.

Catherine felt strange and awkward walking next to Will. She sensed Norman Clare and the other men watching them. 'I'm sorry,' she said, 'I'm sorry, Will. I had to see you. You don't come for me any more like you used to.'

Will stared at the ground. 'Father says there's too much to be done now before winter to go off walking, even if Sir Robert says I'm to.'

Catherine felt a lump in her throat. 'You mean you only showed me all those places because you had to?'

Will stopped walking and looked at her. His voice was suddenly harsh. 'Is that what you really think?'

Catherine looked away. She could feel tears burning her cheeks. Suddenly it was all too much – Sister Anna and everything and now Will like this.

'Catherine, don't, don't,' Will stammered. 'What is it? What's the matter?'

'It's her, it's Sister Anna. I know what happened now. They killed her, the nuns, in the tower. Perhaps she's still there, Will, that's why she comes. Only I don't know whether it's her even, or whether I'm just seeing myself. I can't bear it any more, Will, and now you like this, as though you don't want to see me . . .'

'But I do, I do – You mustn't think that. It's just –'

'Just what?'

'Your uncle, I'm not what he would want, would expect for you.'

'I want to be with you, Will. I want to see you. He can't stop me. Please come and see me, please don't stop coming. I'm frightened, Will, I'm frightened it's all going to happen again.'

Will gently put his arm around her. 'It'll be all right. Nothing's going to happen. I'll come, I promise. I'll try and get away.'

They stayed quietly sitting on the log together, his arm around her. Catherine was resting against him, calmer now. That was how Norman Clare found them a few minutes later.

'It's gone further than I thought,' he muttered to himself.

Catherine and Will jumped up when they saw him.

'Will, get back to the Abbey now,' he said gruffly. 'The wall's got to be finished before dusk. Hurry now. I'll see Miss Catherine safely home.'

Chapter XI

T**HAT NIGHT, WHEN** Will and his father were alone together in the cellar of the White Hart, Norman Clare felt the time had come to speak. He shouldn't have let things get so far.

'She's not for you, Will, do you understand? You're not to see her again.'

'What do you mean, not see her? Sir Robert says . . .'

'Sir Robert's no fool. Although he's given her such free reign, don't you know what he intends? Why do you think he pampers her, gives into her whims, lets her roam about with you. He's sweetening her, getting ready to marry her off, and not to the likes of you. Forget her. What do you think Sir Robert would do if he knew there was anything between you?'

'But there isn't . . . I mean . . .'

'You don't know what you mean. I've seen her looking for you, waiting for you. I'm surprised the poor child hasn't gone mad with loneliness in that awful ruin. Perhaps she might have done but for you. But it isn't our business, it can't be. It was never meant, anything between that family and ours, not after what happened.'

'What are you talking about?'

'Sit down, Will. Perhaps I should have told you before now, before anything even started. Few people know the truth about the Helmsby family, about the Abbey and Count Drogo and what happened there all those years ago. Only a few families know the real truth – it's been passed down from generation to generation.'

'I know about Sister Anna and Count Drogo . . .'

'Let me finish.'

'My father told me, just as his father told him, and his father before that . . . Just as I'm telling you now. But it's a dark secret, a heavy one to bear and it's never to be told beyond this family.'

'What terrible secret? What are you talking about?'

'The fire that killed Count Drogo – it wasn't lightning that started that fire. That was the story put out by the villagers. No one could ever prove otherwise. The fire was started deliberately by four men from this village. One of those men was your great-grandfather.'

'He killed the Count?'

'He and the three others. All driven by madness and grief. They had lost their daughters. Four young girls found dead in the pool below the Abbey.'

'You mean Owen's brides?'

Norman Clare nodded. 'So the Count would have everyone believe. It was he that had young Owen killed. His spies had seen the boy with the Sister Anna. He tortured the truth from him. Owen confessed that the young nun was his bride. Count Drogo used this knowledge to turn the nuns out of the Abbey, and the convent was disbanded. When he had finished with Owen he had him killed too. Owen's body was put in the pool to make it look as though the lovesick boy had drowned himself.

'It was soon after Count Drogo moved into the Abbey that the first girl from the village went missing. She was found a week later, drowned in the same pool. An accidental drowning, or so it seemed at first. But then a second girl was found and then a third. The villagers grew to fear the place and wild stories spread, supernatural tales, put out no doubt by Drogo to suit his own ends. Soon no one dared go near the Abbey or the woods around. It was said that the dead boy's ghost wandered there and had lured the girls to their death.

'And then the miller's daughter went missing. The miller searched for her night and day. He didn't believe the tales – he'd always believed that the Count had had something to do with these dreadful tragedies. For three days and nights he roamed the Abbey grounds, searching for sign or sound of her. One night he thought he heard cries from inside the Abbey. He tried to get in but the Count's men drove him away. He ran down to the pool. He waited there in fearful torment, hoping to the last to save her. Hoping to rescue her when they brought her down. But the poor girl was already dead when the Count's men threw her into the pool.

'What could he do? He knew who had destroyed his child. But what was his word against the powerful Count? He told the other men, the other fathers who'd lost their daughters. They waited and they planned.

'One wild night, when thunder shook the valley and lightning tore the sky in two, the four men crept up to the Abbey. They took the Count and his men by surprise. They dragged them, bound and tied, to the tower and locked them in an upper room. The Count himself would say nothing, but the men confessed, swearing they had been forced to it by the Count. They confessed also to Owen's torture and death. They begged for mercy, but there could be no witnesses. The miller and the other men set the tower alight with their torches. Then they ran back to the village.'

Norman Clare was silent for a moment. 'What they had done was never discovered. By the time help came, the tower was well ablaze and the bodies were burnt beyond recognition. The legends remained: the lightning strike, the brides of Owen ... but each man vowed that the truth about the evil Count and the deaths of their beloved children would not be forgotten. The real truth would be passed down from generation to generation, from father to son, each family sworn to secrecy.'

'But what has this got to do with me and Catherine? It happened a long time ago, it's over,' said Will.

'No,' Norman Clare shouted, 'it's not over. Any link between that family and ours means misery and misfortune. It's not meant to be. Forget her before it's too late, before it starts all over again.'

'I can't forget her. I . . .'

'You're a fool! What did you think Sir Robert had in mind for her – a steward's son for a husband? She's his only way out of here, back to the Court. He intends to marry her off to some nobleman who'll plead his cause with the King. And the sooner the better. Haven't you seen what the place is doing to him? He's half insane, already, according to Joseph. He's seen him at night, leaping round the Abbey, stabbing at the empty air with his sword as though all the devils in hell had come to haunt him. Wake up, Will! Why do you think he's been visiting Lord Osmund? The old fool's just buried his second wife and is probably looking for another.'

Will was white now and trembling. 'She can't marry that . . .'

'She'll do whatever her uncle decides. She'll have no choice.'

'He can't, he can't make her. She doesn't know anything about it, I'm sure. I've got to warn her . . .'

He was filled with a sudden despair, horror. He knew then what Catherine meant to him. He loved her. He wasn't going to let anything happen to her. Suddenly Catherine's nightmares had become his own. He understood. She was right, it was all happening again. The past was stretching out to touch them. He had to see her, had to warn her. He tried to run out of the cellar, but felt his father's arms holding him back.

'No, Will. You're not to go near her, do you hear? It's not our business. You're to stay away from her. You'll make it worse for her. You're not to see her again.'

CHAPTER XII

FOR BOTH CATHERINE and Will the days that followed were a growing horror. For Will they passed in a slow agony: forbidden to go near the Abbey by his father, he was tortured by thoughts of Catherine and Lord Osmund. Obsessed now by the story his father had told him, he knew that the Abbey and its lords were more evil than he had ever imagined. Catherine would never be safe there. Somehow he had to help her.

For Catherine, every minute was taken up with getting ready for entertaining Lord Osmund. Will didn't come as he had promised. Each day she waited for him, hoping to see him. Each day her despair and despondency increased. Perhaps he didn't like her, didn't want to see her. She could think of nothing else.

The preparations became an almost welcome distraction until she began to suspect the reason for her uncle's interest in Lord Osmund. Although he had said nothing to her, was it possible that he wanted her to marry this man? She prayed that she was wrong. Each day passed in a kind of daze. Everything seemed so awful, so unreal — it was as though she was a ghost herself, a shadow with no power over anything. If only she knew whether Will loved her or not.

The morning of Lord Osmund's visit came at last. A huge fire roared in the hall. Roast swan, wild boar and countless pastries were ready in the kitchen and the best wine had been brought up. Catherine and her uncle were waiting by the outer gate when Lord Osmund rode up with two servants. He was a huge, grotesque-looking man with a red beard and bulging eyes. Catherine shuddered. Then, as Sir Robert hurried forward to greet him, Catherine caught sight of Will by the far wall. He was looking towards her. Norman Clare seemed to be holding his arm, trying to pull him away. Her heart leapt. He had come, he did care about her. She felt her uncle take her arm and lead her forward. She glanced back towards Will. He was gone.

Lord Osmund had dismounted now, and was breathing heavily. He took hold of her hand, staring at her in a way which made her uncomfortable. Then he turned away, beaming at her uncle. Catherine was looking beautiful, with her green velvet gown shimmering in the autumn sun, red garnets at her throat and her dark hair falling to her shoulders. Lord Osmund gave her his arm and escorted her into the Abbey.

The feasting seemed to last for ever. Catherine kept thinking about Will. He had come – he had tried to see her. Next to her Lord Osmund drank and belched and leered, stuffing food into his mouth with one hand, his other hand groping for hers. Her head throbbed. She longed for the meal to end and this disgusting creature to be gone so she could look for Will. Her uncle was drinking and smiling. Then at last it was over. With the help of his servants, Lord Osmund staggered to his horse and, with a final kiss of her hand, he was gone.

Catherine turned and ran inside, wanting to be alone, but her uncle followed her. He was brimming over with pleasure and congratulations. 'Well done, my dear. He was completely charmed by you. He's returning next week with the lawyers so the papers can be drawn up. I'm sure you'll be very happy. A fine house and estates at Norton as well as frequent visits to London and the King's Court. He wants to get the matter settled as soon as possible, before the roads became impassable. We shall all be more comfortable there. The sooner the arrangements are made and we leave this dreadful ruin the better. I couldn't have wished for a better marriage. We'll soon be back at Court and my own estates will be restored.'

Catherine felt horribly sick. In a moment she would wake up and everything would be all right again. It had happened so fast. Everything had changed so quickly. Those first few happy weeks with Will and then the growing nightmare, the terrible truth about poor Sister Anna, and now this . . .

'What's the matter, girl? You seem pale and quiet. I expected a little thanks at least for having secured your future so successfully. You'll be mistress of some fine estates.'

'I'm feeling a little ill, Uncle,' said Catherine slowly. 'May I go to my room?'

'Yes, yes. All the excitement and the wine, I expect. Well, you must go and rest now. We'll talk about this again tonight. I have to go to Norton now to see the lawyer.'

Catherine didn't move when Sir Robert left. She sat very quietly, staring at the fire. If she sat very still, perhaps it would all go away.

That was how Will found her some time later. He'd seen Sir Robert riding out of the village. No one would stop him seeing her any more – not his father or Sir Robert or any of them. They weren't going to force her to marry that drunken fool. Somehow he'd look after her. He'd take her away from this awful place. Sir Robert was mad, like Count Drogo – evil and mad. Will would kill him if he had to, just like his great-grandfather had killed Drogo. Nothing was going to hurt Catherine, nothing . . .

Catherine didn't move when Will came into the hall. He walked towards her, calling her softly, but she didn't turn. He knelt down in front of her, anxiously searching her face. He gently took her hands; they were white and cold. The fire had long since gone out.

'Catherine, what is it? What's happened? Have they hurt you?'

At last she looked up at him. She was trembling now and tears were slowly running down her cheeks. He put his arms around her. His own face was wet with tears. He couldn't bear it if anything happened to her.

'It's all right,' he whispered, 'it's all right.'

'I'm to marry Lord Osmund.'

Will felt the blood drain from his face. So his father was right. Catherine was looking intently at him. He shook his head. 'No, you won't marry him. I won't let you. I . . .' He didn't know what to say, how to tell her that he loved her.

But it was Catherine now who took his hand. 'I love you, Will. It's you I want to be with, always.'

'I love you, too.'

Chapter XIII

NEITHER OF THEM heard the door open. He'd been standing there for some time, watching them, listening. They only heard the sharp crack of his whip as he lashed against the stone floor. 'Get out,' Sir Robert hissed at Will. 'Get out of here.'

As he lifted his arm again, Catherine screamed and ran in front of Will. 'No, don't touch him.'

Sir Robert's eyes flashed. He was staring at Will. 'Get out of here,' he screamed.

Will stood his ground. 'I'm not leaving her.'

Sir Robert snorted, his lips curled in mocking fury. He brought the whip down again. 'Get out of here while you still can.'

At that moment the servants, having heard the shouting, burst into the room. He turned on them. 'And all of you – get out now. Get down to the village until I send for you.'

Although by now accustomed to their master's moods and ravings, they'd never seen him like this. He looked more like an animal than a man, with his purple face twisted and distorted, his eyes bulging. He could hardly speak, he spat the words, 'Get out of here now.'

They left quickly. Blanche, unwilling to leave her mistress, was dragged away by Joseph. 'It's best,' he whispered. 'The mood will pass – we'll come back then.'

Martins tried to pull Will away too, but he wouldn't move.

'Didn't you hear me, boy,' screamed Sir Robert again. 'Go! Get out of here before I kill you. Don't ever try to come near her again.'

This time it was Catherine who screamed at Will. 'Go, Will, go now. He won't touch me, he won't hurt me. He wants me for Lord Osmund.'

Will stumbled at last towards the door.

Sir Robert turned back to Catherine. 'That's right. Nobody will touch you, not a hair on your head – unscathed for Lord Osmund, not a scar or a blemish.'

Catherine stared at her uncle, at his angry, livid face. She wasn't frightened, she just felt loathing and contempt. This man who had pretended to befriend her, to show her kindness – where was his warmth now? Where were his sweet, kindly smiles? She felt his sickly breath on her face. 'I won't marry him. You can't make me. I love Will.'

Sir Robert lifted his hand, then checked himself. 'You stupid, stupid girl. You'll do exactly as I tell you. You'll be married to Lord Osmund within the week. How could I have been such a fool? There'll be no moping over that steward's son. You'll be bright and beautiful for Lord Osmund or you'll be sorry – sorry when that boy disappears one dark night and you the cause of it. Do you understand me? I'll have him drowned, put down like a dog if you disobey me.'

Sir Robert was beside himself with rage. Nothing was going to ruin his plans. He would secure this match with Lord Osmund. Nothing, no one would stand in his way. He'd ride there now and bring the date forward. As for Catherine, he'd shut her up in the tower. A night there would bring her to her senses. Let her think about the boy – if she really loved him she wouldn't want him killed.

He took hold of Catherine's arm, dragging her out into the courtyard. She felt strangely tired, unable to run, unable to resist. It all seemed inevitable, played out before. What could she do? Her uncle held all the cards. Will loved her – at least she knew that now – and she loved him, but if she didn't do as her uncle said Will would be destroyed. They reached the tower. Of course, the tower – where else would he take her? She watched as he struggled for a moment with the grille. She couldn't move. She felt herself being grabbed and thrown roughly down the steps into the darkness. She screamed as she fell. She heard her own cry echoing back from the walls. Then there was silence.

CHAPTER XIV

CATHERINE HAD HIT her head when her uncle had thrown her. She'd lain for a long time senseless on the cold steps. It was night before she opened her eyes at last. For a moment she was confused, unable to remember what had happened. She felt very cold and cramped. There was a damp, musty smell. Her head ached. Where was she? The images began to flood slowly back: her uncle dragging her across the courtyard and then her falling and before that Will, Will holding her, telling her he loved her.

It was dark, terribly dark and cold. Behind her she could feel a wall, wet and crumbling, and in front of her some kind of gate, the criss-cross of metal. Her heart began to race. She knew this place. Of course – she was in the tower, her uncle had put her there. This was the metal grille she had once tried to lift, but now she was behind it; she was trapped.

Catherine tried to breathe slowly, pushing down her fear. Her uncle had put her here, but she wasn't going to die. She wasn't going to die like Sister Anna. Will loved her and she was going to be with him again. Somehow she would find a way out. Her eyes became gradually accustomed to the gloom, and she realized that she was lying on a narrow stone ledge. Below her she could see more steps leading downwards. Perhaps there was another way out, a tunnel leading from an underground chamber? Perhaps she could find a piece of wood or iron to use as a lever on the grille. Catherine knew she couldn't lift it on her own; there was no point in trying, she must save her strength. She felt strangely calm. It was as though the worst had happened and she had nothing more to fear. She was here now, shut in the tower like Sister Anna. Everything that she had feared had happened. What else could hurt her? Will loved her, that was all that mattered. The ghosts, the crumbling walls, the deathly silence had no power over her now.

She began to make her way slowly down the damp, spiralling steps. She came at last to a low door set in the rock. She pushed against it; it swung open. More steps led down into a single lonely chamber. Catherine knew at once what she had found. She didn't scream, she stood very still. She stood there for what seemed an eternity. It was as though this horror had been rehearsed a hundred times. Her mind had conjured up this final moment so often that now she felt only numbness.

A coffin stood in the middle of the room. It was open. Its black velvet drapes were mottled green and crumbling with age. By its side, in this most terrible resting place, lay Sister Anna. Her trailing white habit was now crumbling to dust, its remnants still clinging to her long-dead bones. Her skull stared upwards, half smiling now in death.

Catherine walked slowly forwards. So here at last was Sister Anna, Owen's long-lost bride. Catherine took off her own cloak and laid it gently over the poor dead girl. Then she knelt down and began to pray – whether for Sister Anna or for herself, she no longer knew.

After a time, Catherine thought she heard a voice, someone calling her name, but she didn't move. Perhaps it wasn't a voice at all, just the wind whistling through the tower. Then she saw a light and shadows flickering on the wall in front of her. She felt strong arms lifting her up. It was Will.

'I've found you. Thank God, I've found you. I'll never lose you again. We'll be together always. They can't stop us now.'

He tried to help her up, but Catherine struggled free, pulling at his arm. 'Look, Will, look! Sister Anna. We can't leave her.'

She felt Will holding her face again, pleading with her. 'No, Catherine, no. We must go now, before he returns. We'll come back for her, I promise.' Will put his cloak around Catherine and led her gently back up the steps. She was shivering now, but when they reached the entrance the fresh air seemed to revive her. Dawn was already streaking the sky.

'Wait here,' Will told her. 'I've got to put the grille back. It may give us more time.'

Will was back by her side in a moment. 'We've got to go quickly. Can you manage the steep path?'

Catherine nodded. Hand in hand they began to make their way down the rough path towards the village.

Sir robert returned from Lord Osmund's later that morning. Everything had been decided and the papers were now drawn up: the marriage would take place the following day. He just hoped that Catherine had come to her senses after a night on her own. He crossed the courtyard and entered the crumbling tower. With some difficulty he managed to lift the grille. He was pleased that he'd thought to bring a light – the ghastly gloom and silence of the place chilled him. He would be glad when they'd left the Abbey for good.

Sir Robert had expected to find Catherine waiting where he'd left her. 'Drat the girl,' he thought, peering down into the darkness. 'Catherine, where are you, Catherine? It's your uncle come to fetch you. I hope you're sorry for all the trouble you've caused. Come along, Catherine. Come and see the necklace Lord Osmund has sent you.'

Receiving no reply, Sir Robert became increasingly irritated. 'Come out now, girl, do you hear me?'

He began to make his way cautiously down the dark stone steps, the flickering candle making little impression on the growing darkness. He groped his way at last to the open doorway which led to Sister Anna's cell and down the steps. He was more used to the dark now and could just make out something on the floor. The wretched girl was lying down. Had she fallen asleep? What was she playing at? 'Catherine, get up,' he screamed. 'I'm not waiting any longer.'

He crept nearer and took hold of the edge of Catherine's cloak. 'Get up, do you hear?' He pulled away the cloak. The smiling skull grinned white out of the darkness. Sister Anna smiled her sweet revenge.

Sir Robert staggered backwards. He opened his mouth to scream, but no sound came from his lips. He clutched his throat. A hundred thoughts ripped through his mind. Catherine dead? What ghastly devilment was this? Was he completely mad? He stumbled blindly up the stone steps, crashing his head into the low doorway. The force of the blow threw him backwards into the cell again. He fell, still clutching the candle, into the open coffin.

It was a tiny flame at first, a golden flicker. The rotten wood and black velvet drapes caught first, the smouldering dust spitting and sparkling as the flames grew and the smoke curled upwards. Sir Robert Helmsby lay still. The flames crept over him, licking his cloak, his boots, his unkempt beard. Slowly the fire grew, seeking whatever it could, whatever would still burn within the tower.

They saw the flames from the village, but by the time they reached the Abbey, the fire was spent and the last Lord of the Abbey was dead.

Catherine inherited the estate, and the following spring she and Will were married. Sister Anna was buried in the churchyard, beside the grave of Owen.

'She won't trouble us any more,' said Will. 'She's at rest now. Owen has found his bride at last.'

As Catherine and Will climbed back towards the Abbey, the stones shone white and tranquil in the sunlight. A pair of wood doves called to each other from the outer gate, tiny wrens crept through the ivy and thrushes and blackbirds sang from the surrounding trees. Deer grazed by the Abbey walls and a small lizard warmed itself in the spring sunshine. The Abbey had lost its ghosts.

Also in the **DARK ENCHANTMENT** series

The Hounds of Winter
by LOUISE COOPER

CHAPTER I

A T THE MOMENT when Silvan put the ring on Tavia's finger, Jansie simply couldn't bear to watch but turned her head away, furiously biting back the tears. *Silvan doesn't love me,* she told herself. *He loves my sister, and today is their wedding day, and I must forget my dreams!*

The priest spoke the final words, and a little sigh went through the gathering of family and friends. Husband and wife. Silvan and Tavia. And as she looked at the tall, dark, gauntly handsome figure of her new brother-in-law, Jansie felt as if a knife had stabbed into her heart.

With the ceremony over, the celebration began. The house had been decorated with ribbons, garlands and good-luck symbols; a hundred candles burned in the great hall, and everywhere was brightness and laughter. All Jansie's relations had come, uncles and aunts and cousins, and many friends besides; enough people to make up for the fact that Silvan had no family of his own. Later there was music and dancing, and soon after the dancing began, Jansie's cousin Issa found Jansie sitting alone on the landing that overlooked the great staircase.

'Oh, Jansie!' Issa crouched down, her face sympathetic and concerned. 'Please don't cry.'

'I'm not crying,' Jansie said fiercely. But it wasn't true; tears were glittering on her eyelashes.

'It's Silvan, isn't it?' Issa sighed. 'The trouble is, I think every girl who ever sets eyes on him must fall in love with him.'

'Don't tell Tavia, Issa, please don't!' Jansie pleaded. 'I don't want to spoil her day.'

'Of course I won't tell her,' Issa said. She knew how fond Jansie and Tavia had always been of each other.

'And I am being foolish, I know,' Jansie went on mournfully. 'Tavia's three years older than me, and Silvan's older still. I'm too young for him – Mother says I shouldn't even be thinking about marriage until I'm at least seventeen, and that's two years away. But oh, Issa, it doesn't stop me *wishing*.'

'I know.' Issa sighed again. Then, trying to buoy Jansie with a wry joke, she added, 'Perhaps Silvan has a younger brother? Or two would be better — then we could have one each!'

Jansie almost managed to laugh, then shook her head. 'Silvan hasn't got any family at all.' And she thought silently, *Except for Tavia. She's his family now. And tonight she'll go away with him, away to his house, where they'll both be so far from me . . .*

'Come on,' Issa said, seeing that Jansie was about to cry again. 'You mustn't go back with red eyes and blotchy cheeks, or Tavia *will* know that you're upset. Let me dab your face — there, that's better — and we'll go downstairs together.' She pulled her cousin to her feet and linked arms firmly with her. 'You'll get over him, Jansie. You will.'

The carriage that was to take Silvan and Tavia away to their new life was at the door shortly after sunset. All the guests gathered on the steps to wish them Godspeed on their four-day journey, and Tavia, radiant and laughing, swept Jansie into her arms.

'Oh, Jansie, this has been such a wonderful day!' Tavia hugged her sister tightly. 'Now, you'll come and see us soon, won't you? Promise?'

'I promise. As soon as you want me to come, just write to me.' And Jansie meant it. For until she was invited, until that letter came, there would be no chance to see Silvan again.

Then Silvan stepped forward. He took Jansie's hands in his and she felt a thrill rush through her fingers, through her arms, into her heart. She looked up at his face, at the fine bones, the frame of black hair with the strange but distinguishing white streak at the temples. Into his vivid green eyes . . .

Silvan smiled at her, a smile that devastated her soul. 'Goodbye, dear sister Jansie,' he said. And Jansie's dreams collapsed and blew away on the late summer breeze. *Sister*. That was all she was to him, all she would ever be. He loved Tavia. And that hurt so much.

She heard the carriage door close, heard the coachman call to the horses — 'Come *hup*!' — and the crack of the whip. Hoofs clattered, the carriage wheels rumbled, and Silvan and Tavia were carried away into the gathering night.

Jansie went up to her bedroom. The festivities were still in full swing and would go on until past midnight, but she couldn't bear to join in any more. She closed her door and sat down in front of her looking-glass, gazing at her own face. Her hair wasn't golden like Tavia's, but only brown. And her eyes were not blue, only hazel. *Tavia is beautiful*, Jansie thought, *and I'm not*. Little wonder that Silvan had fallen in love with her sister. Little wonder that he would never dream of looking twice at Jansie . . .

Suddenly Jansie couldn't face the glass any more. She ran to her bed, threw herself down on the familiar, friendly counterpane, and sobbed herself to sleep.

Tavia wrote once to say that she and Silvan had arrived safely, and then there was no further letter for months. Summer gave way to autumn and autumn to winter, and still no word came. Jansie fretted more and more each week, until her father despaired of her and even her mother declared that she was becoming 'quite impossible!'

Then, a few days after the Midwinter Solstice, a letter came. It wasn't brought by the usual post-runner but by a fair-haired boy some two or three years older than Jansie, who rode up to the door on a stout pony one brisk, chilly morning. The boy's name was Gilmer, he said; he was in service at Silvan's house and his master had asked him to carry this message. Jansie barely gave the young messenger a second glance; she was too excited and eager to know what Tavia had to say.

But the letter wasn't from Tavia. It was from Silvan himself. He had to go away on business, he said, and would be absent from home until spring. He was worried that Tavia would be lonely, and so he wondered if Jansie might wish to stay at his house during his absence, to keep her sister company.

Jansie was thrilled by the invitation, but underlying the thrill was a feeling of great disappointment. She had missed Tavia greatly during the past few months ... but stronger than the desire to see her sister again was the desire to see Silvan. Though Jansie had tried to forget her longings, her efforts had been futile. She still dreamed of Silvan each night, still thought of him each day. And now, when the long-awaited invitation had finally come, he would not be there. It seemed a bitterly cruel blow.

But if she would not see Silvan himself, she thought, at least she would see his house, and that prospect fascinated her. So the following day she set out, with Gilmer as escort.

The morning was bright but cold, with frost glittering on the hedgerows and a fresh, chill snap to the wind. The ponies' hoofs rang and echoed cheerfully on the road, and as they trotted along, Jansie looked sidelong at her companion. Gilmer had a charming manner, she thought. Handsome, too – though in a very different way from Silvan, for Gilmer was smaller, slim without being gaunt, and had warm grey eyes and thick fair hair in which the winter sun made rainbows of colour. He was obviously attracted to Jansie, and she knew that if circumstances had been different she might well have been drawn to him. But each time she looked at Gilmer, the shadow of Silvan moved across her inner vision. It was wrong, Jansie *knew* it was wrong. But her brother-in-law had snared her heart, and she could have no thought for anyone else.

They did talk a great deal on the journey, however, and Jansie soon learned that Gilmer was no ordinary servant. He came from an old, respected and once-wealthy family, but in recent years they had fallen on hard times. Gilmer knew a great deal about herbalism and his ambition was to become a physician. But such training cost money, and so Gilmer now worked for Silvan, as his steward. Soon they were laughing and talking like old friends.

'Well, Jansie, I'm glad to hear you so cheerful despite the cold!' Gilmer dropped the reins for a moment and rubbed his hands together. 'Winter's early this year, and it looks set to be a bitter one. We even had a snowfall on the Winter Solstice, and that's very rare – in fact I don't think it's happened before in my father's lifetime, let alone in mine.'

'You mean you don't get snow?' Jansie was surprised.

'Oh yes, we do, but usually not until a month after the Solstice is past. The forest where we – that is, where your sister and brother-in-law live is very sheltered. Cool in the summer, warm in the winter. Only this year the weather seems to have something else in mind. A few days ago, I even heard –' Then, as though thinking better of it, he broke off abruptly.

Jansie looked at him, curious. 'What did you hear?'

'Oh, nothing.' But there was a strange expression on Gilmer's face. 'It isn't important.'

But it was. Jansie could tell. And as they rode on, suddenly silent, she felt a sense of creeping unease begin to form somewhere very deep in her mind . . .